CW00863862

The Adventures of Mandy:

Panda Lost at Sea

by Michele S Vermeulen

© 2017 Michele S Vermeulen

The Adventures of Mandy:

PANDA

Lost at Sea!

Written & Illustrated by

Michele S Vermeulen

CHAPTER 1

Mandy was loved. She knew this by her worn coat and the plaster that covered her left eye. She was not plump and fluffy like the others that sat on the end of Anna's bed, plush, soft and new. Instead her fur was worn and scruffy, and her stuffing had long thinned, her arms floppy from

5

being dragged along, and her nose torn where it had been chewed over the years. But Mandy knew she was loved, for she was Anna's favourite panda. She was the one Anna always went to for cuddles when she hurt her knee. She was the one Anna hugged tight at night when she was afraid of the dark. And she was the one Anna took on many adventures. While all the others sat quietly at the end of the bed hoping to be picked, it was Mandy she always chose as her

companion, and who she cried
for when she was sad.

Adventures with Anna were
the best part of being her
favourite panda, and Mandy
had been lucky enough to have
had many. She had been to

the supermarket, where she had got to ride in a trolley, and to the park, where she had been on the slide, the swings and the roundabout. Mandy loved her adventures with Anna, at least until one day when Mandy's thrill for adventure took her too far……

That morning there had been quite the flurry of activity at home as mum, dad, Kieron and Anna were all preparing to go on holiday.

'Bags? Check!' said Kieron.

'Snacks? Check! 'said mum.

'Mandy? Check!' said Anna.

Mandy sat snuggled in the back of Anna's rucksack, her head peeping out the top as Anna climbed in to the back of the car.

'We're going on holidays, yippee!' Anna and Kieron squealed with delight as the car pulled off the drive and headed towards the ferry port in Dover, where they would cross for their two-week holiday by the sea.

'Now kids, once we board we can go out on deck and see the sea', dad told them as the car crawled along its lane, following the direction of the attendant as they boarded the ferry.

The ship was huge, a giant tank on water, its colossal chains holding gigantic anchors pinned firmly to the bottom of the sea and steadying the hatch as the cars, lorries, vans and campers all rolled into place. Mandy peered out from

Anna's rucksack, the dark echoing bowels of the ship drumming through her ears. It was exciting, but somewhat frightening too. Mandy huddled in Anna's rucksack, eyes now shut. She would be glad when she was safely on

deck and in Anna's arms again.

Mandy bounced up and down in Anna's bag as she made her way up the numerous steps, past the parking levels and on to the passenger deck of the ship. The gangways were alive with people, some heading towards the lounge, some to the games room, and some just standing around wondering which way to go. Anna followed mum, dad and Kieron towards a large door that lead to the outside deck, her rucksack hanging over both shoulders, Mandy's head visible at the top as she stepped out to a glorious sight.

The deck was washed white and had lifeboats with bright orange covers dotted all along the side of the ship. There was seating with many

now enjoying the view of the port and the other boats of varying sizes that were anchored up and down the coast line. Mandy was mesmerised by the sight of the vast ocean, big and beautiful, the sun shimmering on its surface, gently lapping against the side of the ship, and stretching as far as the eye could see. She thought about what she would tell the others left behind on Anna's bed. This really had to be her ultimate adventure, so she climbed out of Anna's rucksack and sat up on her shoulders to get a better view.

Suddenly there was a loud noise, the ship was on the move. Its horn echoed across the port and out to sea, telling the world it was coming, as it slowly made its way out of the harbour and into the great wide open. The waves were bigger here, and the boat now bobbed up and down as the wind started to pick up and the sky darkened.

'It looks like it's going to rain' said mum, 'why don't

we head inside for a warm drink?'

They made their way towards the door when suddenly, a huge gust of wind took them by surprise, and sent Mandy tumbling from Anna's shoulders.

'Mandy!' Anna cried as dad dived to catch her, but the wind blew Mandy across the deck.

She tried to find a place to hold on but her soft worn paws had no grip so she rolled helplessly in the wind.

'Mandy!' Anna now hysterical as dad chased Mandy along the deck, hand out, but each time missing her as another gust carried her further away, and under the railings towards the edge of the ship.

Frightened, Mandy tried her best to hold on, waiting for dad to come to her rescue, her limp body now hanging halfway out to sea.

'Mandy!' Anna continued to cry, now from inside the doorway where mum had taken her and Kieron to safety.

Mandy watched as dad stretched his arm out between the railings towards her, but it was no use, the wind was too strong for a scraggly little panda like her. With the next gust, the wind sent her sailing up into the sky and out to sea. She watched as she was carried through the air, eyes on Anna, who was now standing helplessly in the doorway, tears rolling down her cheeks, calling for her beloved Mandy. Down Mandy fell into the vast ocean, waves engulfing her, and carrying her further and further away from Anna. She gasped as the cold water hit her, soaking into her fur and drenching her from head to toe. Mandy, now treading water amidst the giant waves, watched silently as the ship moved away, becoming smaller

21

smaller, and eventually disappearing over the horizon.

CHAPTER 2

Mandy was lost. She wept bitterly as she thought of her family back on the ship; she so desperately wanted to be with them, enjoying a warm drink in the comfort of Anna's arms. Why had she got out of the rucksack? If she had stayed safely inside she wouldn't be here right now, on her own, in the big sea, lost. She hung in the water, her tired arms and legs moving to keep her afloat, but growing weaker with every stroke. She was, after all, just a scraggly little panda, her limp arms no match for the great sea. With every wave, she could feel her strength failing, until at last she gave in to the blue and let herself be engulfed by the water.

Under the waves the sea was much calmer. She silently drifted down, allowing the current to sway her gently. She knew eventually she would reach the bottom of the ocean, her worn fur sodded with water, too heavy to float. Mandy knew that wherever she landed, she would spend the rest of her days, eventually gathering algae and slime, and maybe even becoming home to a small sea creature. Sometimes she wished she were a real panda, at least then she could have held on tighter to the railings when the wind came, or if she had still fallen in, she might have been able to swim back to the ship.

Mandy thought about Anna, her arms outstretched, tears

spilling down her face as she called for her. She worried about how Anna would sleep at night without her, willing herself to be found, by some miracle, there in the middle of the sea. But as Mandy sank beneath the waves something brushed underneath her, sending her tumbling once more, but this time into a swirling surge of water, before pushing her upwards towards the surface again.

Mandy broke through the waves, soared high into the air and then down again with an almighty splash, before slowly settling on the surface. She looked down and saw beneath her what appeared to be a large barnacle-encrusted rock, now elongated in the water. Suddenly there was another surge of water, and Mandy shot up high into the air again, a fountain of water pushing her upwards, then falling away and sending her tumbling back down again.

'I'm getting too old for this', she thought wearily and then noticed a large eye peering up at her from the side of the rock.

'You are not a rock, are you?' she said.

'No, my dear I am not, and you are not a fish', it replied.

'My name is Mandy, and I am lost', she said.

'I am a great whale of the ocean, and I think you don't belong here. You need to go home'.

'Oh yes, yes, please, I must find my Anna!' cried Mandy. 'You see she is my best cuddle friend and I miss her terribly, and she can't sleep without me. The wind was too strong, and I was blown off the ship and was tumbling down into the blue and I couldn't swim…' Mandy continued.

'OK, my furry friend, slow down', said the whale 'unlike you, whales are great swimmers. I will take you where you need to go little one'.

Mandy's heart lifted, and for the first time since her saga began she saw hope of being reunited with her beloved Anna.

'I must get to holidays', she thought.

The whale steadied on the surface of the water while Mandy found a comfortable spot.

'You may be in for quite a ride little one, so do hold on tight. Now, where do you want to go?'.

'I need to go to holidays!' exclaimed Mandy, 'that is where Anna has gone and that is where I will find her'.

'Holidays?' quizzed the whale, 'I don't think I know that place. Is it a land place?'

Mandy thought for a moment 'a land place is not a sea place so it must be. Yes, it is a land place', she said firmly.

The whale knew of land places but had never been. She had always kept away from the coastlines. She had heard the stories of whales swimming too close and getting stuck in the sand, and it frightened her.

'I know of land places my friend but they are not for whales. I can take you some of the way but I must stay in the deep blue, or I will get stuck in the sand', she said.

'OK,' said Mandy, 'take me as far as you can.'

Mandy wondered what she would do when she got as far as the whale could go, but

for now she would try to be
happy that she was at least
on her way. She was no
longer sure which way the
ferry had gone, as all
directions look the same in
the middle of the ocean.
However, she trusted the
whale and her excellent ears
that now followed the
underwater whirring of a
distant ship.

CHAPTER 3

Mandy was excited. She sailed happily on the whales back, the wind blowing round her ears as she bumped up and down with every wave. She took in the sights and smells of the ocean, passing schools of fish and occasionally being accompanied by a pod of dolphins. They leapt gracefully through the water, their sleek bodies shaped like tubes darting in and out, as they eyed the little black and white shape riding on the back of the whale. Mandy marvelled at these wonderful creatures, their bright eyes staring curiously as they flew over her, swimming in zigzag, and squealing and whistling playfully as they went.

'You're funny', they giggled, as they pushed and shoved one another to get the best spot next to the whale,

and as near to Mandy as possible.

'Can you ride on my back for a while?' one asked, before being bottle-nosed out of the way by his big brother clicking 'I'm first!'

'No, me!' squealed another.

'No one is getting a turn,' scolded the whale, 'the panda stays with me', and the cheeky dolphins sped off in front before turning and springing over her, soaking Mandy as they went.

The whale swam on for what seemed like hours, until at last she slowed when land came in to sight over the horizon.

'This is as far I can go my little friend', she said mournfully.

'But the coast is miles away, however will I get there?' said Mandy sadly.

'You will need to see if you can hitch a ride from a smaller creature, one who can go closer to the land and won't get beached in the sand', said the whale.

'But who? There's nothing but sea for miles!' cried Mandy.

'Aah, my little land one, the sea is full of creatures that can help you, don't be disheartened', said the whale.

Mandy thought about the pod of dolphins that had swam with them for several hours but had long lost interest in her and gone in search of fish.

'If only I had thought to ask them if they would help me', she thought, 'maybe they could have brought me closer to the shore'.

The fear and sadness returned, and she began to think that she would never see her Anna again. Sensing her sorrow, the whale rocked from side to side, a game they had played to while away the hours since their journey had begun. Mandy had loved the game, and it had sent her into fits of laughter as she slid from side to side on the great whales back. But this time it was no use, nothing could lift Mandy's spirits now. The whale hated to see her weary little friend so sad, and without warning she dived under the waves, sending Mandy tumbling once again, as she headed towards the depths.

'Are you holding on', she asked Mandy, who had managed to steady herself against the surge of water that had pulled at her as the whale descended.

She nodded weakly as she clasped the whale's fin, which now speeded through the water towards a large meadow of sea grass and algae clustered at the bottom of the sea. As the whale neared she slowed and then carefully cruised around the edges. The sea grass was full of life. Multi-coloured fish

hovered amongst the green stems, dashing and darting in and out, chattering noisily, their numerous colours shimmering in the sun that broke through the surface far above. Crabs scuttled hastily along the sea floor in search of hiding places in the long grass, and under rocks that had formed in the sea bed, squabbling over each spot.

'Get outta here!' shouted one, as another scurried under a large rock which was covered in algae.

Mandy couldn't believe how many different animals lived beneath the waves, and were congregating at this busy little spot for a feast. Manatees, octopus, cuttlefish and sea turtles, all elbowing their way past one another in search of the best roots.

The whale slowly swam closer to the meadow, the sea creatures too busy to notice the enormous mammal coming up behind them. However, the surge made by her giant body was now beginning to disturb the waters, causing some of the roots to break and float away with the current. A crab on the move that had spied the perfect spot stopped dead in its tracks when it saw the whale approaching.

'Whoa! What is that', his pincer now pointing upwards, causing all of the others to turn and look at the colossal creature now before them.

A mass of hysteria ensued.

'Stop, you can't come any closer, you'll destroy the meadow, and probably some of us with it', said a stingray that had been hovering near the edge of the meadow.

'Yo dude, what gives?' asked a sea turtle, 'you know it's really not cool for you to swim so close to our patch'.

'I know', said the whale, 'I am sorry, but I have made a promise to a little friend of mine and cannot break it. I have a favour to ask,' she said to the sea turtle, and as she lowered her head, Mandy came into view on top.

'Whoa!' said the crab again, 'you don't look like a sea animal!'

'I am not' said Mandy sadly, 'for I was lost at sea until my friend the whale rescued me. I just want to go home'.

Mandy told them the whole story, and explained about holidays and the land place and how the whale couldn't go too close in case she was beached in the sand. The sea creatures gasped as they listened to Mandy's tale, of how she had lost Anna because she had wanted to see the view from her shoulders and how her excitement had landed her in the middle of the ocean.

'Far out dude', said the sea turtle, 'I can go on land, I will take you to holidays!' he announced.

Mandy sat slouched over the whale's back, her stuffing so sodden with water she could barely move.

'We need to get you out of the water little one', said the whale.

The sea turtle breezed over next to her as the whale tilted to one side, allowing the swollen panda to slide off her back and on to the turtle's. Mandy pulled herself up to the rim of his shell, her paws clutching on as tightly as she could as the turtle saluted his friends before taking off for the surface.

'So long', called Mandy to the whale, 'and thank you for helping me. I will never forget your kindness…' she trailed as the turtle broke water and the world below disappeared beneath the waves.

Mandy lay on his back, her drenched body now seeping water and lightening the weight of her coat.

'I will try my best to keep you out of the water', he said, 'but the shark dudes are pretty fierce and would like to make a snack of me. I may need to dive down into the blue sometimes.'

Mandy nodded and then lay her weary head on the turtles back and fell asleep.

Mandy woke to the frantic cries of the turtle.

'SHARK!' he shrieked before diving under the water.

His pace was rapid as he darted up and down, zigzagging between rocks and seaweed, in hope of losing the shark that was now following closely, snapping at his flippers. Mandy held on as tightly as she could, edging up the turtles back to avoid the chomping, snapping, crunching and grinding of the shark's teeth.

'I will have you for my lunch, a juicy land creature is very good to eat', he snarled.

'But I am not a real land animal, I am a panda teddy, Anna's panda teddy!' Mandy cried in terror, 'if you catch me my stuffing will come out and I will never get home'.

The shark was not interested in the feeble cries of a land animal.

'These herbivores are all the same', he thought,

'they'll say anything to get out of it!'

The shark glided over the rocks, swooping and swerving as he gave chase, the sea turtle flipping and dodging, trying to outwit him with every turn. But he was beginning to tire and worried that maybe this time he would not make it. At that moment, when he thought all hope was lost, he saw the familiar coral that told him land was near, the sand now coming up to meet him as the water got shallower and shallower with every swish of his flippers. He swam with all his might until Mandy emerged from the water as they reached the beach. The shark fast behind them came skidding along the sand, his fin thrashing frantically as he realised he had overshot the waves and was now wriggling helplessly on the beach.

'Phew, that was close, I thought we were gonners for sure!' he said as he waddled up the beach.

'You did it', said Mandy, 'you got me to holidays! Thank you so much', and she lay down on the beach, exhausted, but very glad to be back on solid ground.

CHAPTER 4

Mandy was weary. She had dosed off on the beach and woke to the sound of seagulls circling above, the hot sun beating down on her, drying her fur and the soggy stuffing inside her. She had been saved from the sea, and for that she would be eternally grateful to her new friends, but now she needed to find Anna. She knew that the children came to the beach when they were at holidays, and as she had found the beach, figured it would only be a matter of time before they came to play.

Mandy waited, and waited, and waited, but no children came to the beach. In fact, no humans at all came to the beach. Instead it was awash with seaweed, and alive with

the noisy gaggling of gulls
and barking of sea lions.

'So when do the people
come?' she asked the sea
turtle who was now preparing
to go back to the sea.

'What people?' he asked puzzled.

'The humans, the people at holidays. When do they come to build sand castles?' she asked.

Mandy knew all about sand castles, she had been left in the sand pit at the back of the garden many a time when Anna had excitedly played with her bucket and spade. She knew that Anna and Kieron loved the sand and was sure that they would come to the beach.

'Humans? For real?' replied the turtle, 'I've never seen humans come to this beach, although there are plenty of other critters that come to feed and lay their eggs. When you said you needed to get to the beach, I brought you to the beach, you didn't say which one my friend.'

Mandy was puzzled, 'you mean there is more than one of these beaches?'

'Why hell yes dude, there are beaches everywhere, hundreds of 'em at every coast!' the turtle exclaimed.

'Hundreds of them', she thought, 'at every coast'.

Her heart sank. How would she ever find her family? Her face in her paws she closed her eyes and wept for the second time since her journey began.

'I just want to go home', she said, 'I just want my family back'.

The sea turtle sidled up next to her.

'Cheer up', he said, 'at least we made it here and you are among friends. Maybe you could build yourself a nest by the rocks there'.

Mandy looked up at him, her sorrow turning to anger, 'what good is that if I can't find Anna!' she said.

'Whoa, chill out', said the turtle, 'there are more beaches, if you want to keep looking; it was only a suggestion. We can start with the one over the dunes there, they have people.'

'What?' said Mandy, 'you mean just over there?'

'Yup', he said.

'You mean just over the top of that dune there?' she said.

'Yes, that's what I just said isn't it!' replied the turtle.

'Well what are we sitting here for? Let's go', shrieked Mandy.

'Hold your horses now little panda, you can't just go to a beach full of humans. Think about it, what will they think if some turtle dude turns up with a black and white panda sitting on his back? I'll tell you what, they'll think we're weird; and ready for the zoo!' said the turtle.

'No, we have to go back out to sea and I will somehow have to get you close enough so you can drift in. You'll be washed up to shore where Anna will see you and job done, you're on the home stretch matey!'

Once again Mandy clambered on to the turtles' back, and when he was sure she was holding on, he dived into the

waves and headed out to sea
again.

CHAPTER 5

Mandy held on tight. The sea turtle bounced up and down through the waves until he had passed the last group of rocks before turning left to go around them, and heading back inland again towards the beach. This time the beach was littered with umbrellas and sun loungers, wind breakers and sand castles, and of course people. Humans of all shapes and sizes enjoying the sunshine, with rugs and picnic baskets, and parasols protecting them from the scorching heat. Everywhere little boys and little girls built sand castles, scooping up the sand and filling their buckets, collecting shells and decorating their masterpieces.

'That would be Anna and Kieron', she thought, 'they

love the sand and would make the most amazing castles'.

Mandy's heart raced at the thought of being reunited with them, how overjoyed they would be at seeing her again, and how marvellous that she had managed to come all this way having been lost at sea.

The sea turtle stopped swimming and hovered in the water. Nearby, there were several canoes with holidaymakers paddling in the water, some novices, trying their best to master canoeing, a skill they would most likely not re-use once the holiday was over; and others were experts, demonstrating their abilities with agility and finesse.

'This is as far as I go dude', said the turtle.

'I understand', said Mandy, although she knew the minute she climbed off the turtles back she would sink to the bottom of the sea. He saw the anguish in her eyes and knew that she would be stranded if he left her there, so close to the shore, but far enough away to still be lost at sea.

'OK', he sighed, 'to the crest of the first wave, but you better make sure you can surf dude!'

'I will, I will', she promised, hope rising once again in her weary little heart.

The sea turtle swam on, he knew he could not abandon this helpless little land creature, she had come so far. He knew also in his heart that the world was full of beaches, and he had seen many in his 50 years of swimming the seas, and would most likely see many more in the years to come. But he realised that Mandy needed to believe that she would find her Anna, that she would be reunited once again with her family, there on that beach. Deep down, he hoped that for her too, or at least if not her family, she would find another that would love her as deeply as they did.

The sea turtle approached the wave as it began to swell and rise, the full power of the ocean and the will of all those creatures who had met Mandy on her perilous journey, culminating in a single wave, a wave that would carry her back to safety and back to her home.

'Are you ready?' he whispered as the wave grew higher and higher.

'I am' she replied, trying to hide the fear mounting in her throat.

The sea turtle swam towards it as the wave reached its peak, its crest now towering above them, majestic and sublime. Mandy stared up at it in wonder, the power and the beauty of the sea there before her. The turtle made a sudden movement, flipping to one side and sending Mandy hurtling into the water.

'Good luck my friend, remember…'

Mandy could just make out the first few words of what he said, the rush of the wave was too loud as the crest rose magnificently like a great wall of sea.

'Thank you', she mouthed but could not hear her own words as she watched him disappear through the wave and was gone.

Mandy gazed up silently and in awe as she saw the wave begin to tumble, crashing down towards her, engulfing everything in its path. She braced herself and closed her little eyes as she was sent tumbling uncontrollably into the foam.

It was like being in a washing machine, her head spinning as she was tossed round and round, bouncing on the sea bed as she moved at lightning speed towards the shore. And then finally, the wave started to subside and slow, its power spent as it crawled through the shallow waters, carrying Mandy with it and washing her up on to the sand.

Mandy had made it, somehow, she had made it. She lay helpless and exhausted for the second time on a beach, but this time it was not without people. This time the shoreline was littered with them, and she hoped with all her little heart, that one of those people was Anna.

CHAPTER 6

Mandy had reached holidays. She was beaten and worn, but she had made it. She lay silently in the sand, her fur even more scraggly and her stuffing thinner than when her journey had begun. She could hear the laughter of children playing, their voices shrieking with delight as they splashed in and out of the water; the slop and slosh of the wet sand as they filled their buckets and ferried it to the towering castles they had built further up the beach; and the soothing lap of the waves as they sprawled out over the shore.

Mandy lay there waiting to be found, little feet pitter-pattering around her, busying themselves with sandcastle making, wave dodging, ice cream eating,

shell collecting and panda
teddy finding….

'Look at this!' shrieked a boy as he towered over Mandy, his shadow blocking the scorching sun that had been beating down on her.

Soon she was surrounded by a group of small children, each as curious as the next, as they poked and prodded and kicked the scraggly old panda lying washed up on the shore.

'Ah, it's nothing,' said an older girl, 'just some smelly old panda teddy that someone must have thrown away and it ended up in the sea.'

Disappointed, the children dispersed, making their way back to their sand castles and their shells. But further up the beach a little girl was running. Sprinting as fast as she could down towards the little black and white heap that lay sodden, and tangled in seaweed by the edge of the water. Behind her was a little boy, somewhat older than her but he too was making his way towards the discovery. The children had heard the commotion, and the words 'panda teddy' had carried on the wind, up the beach, to where they had been building a dam in the sand. A panda teddy that had been washed up to shore; it had to be, there was no other possibility, it simply had to be Mandy...

Mum and dad were now in pursuit as Anna and Kieron dodged their way through the blankets and towels, parasols and windbreakers that littered the beach. When they reached the shoreline, they stopped dead in their tracks, mum and dad nearly knocking them over as they took the last windbreaker too quickly, and came grinding to a very abrupt halt.

Anna's heart was racing at a thousand miles per hour. She slowly approached the soggy lump that lay in the sand. She was afraid to look for she could not bear the heartbreak of losing Mandy again. She edged closer and bent down over it.

'Pick it up Anna', a voice came from behind, her

decisive brother urging her to get on with the job.

'I'm scared Kieron, what if it isn't Mandy,' she said.

He sidled up next to her and took her hand, 'it's ok', he said, squeezing it slightly, 'pick it up'.

Eyes on Kieron, Anna reached down and picked up the ball of matted black and white fur and turned it over.

'MANDY!!!!!' she squealed 'Mandy!'. Anna squeezed the teddy so tightly that water drenched from its soaked fur and dripped down all over her.

'I found you!' she cried, tears now pouring down her cheeks as her heart swelled with joy. 'I found you!'.

Anna had found her Mandy. Tattered, smelly and more worn, but Mandy all the same. Kieron, mum and dad crowded around her, equally as overjoyed to see Anna reunited with her favourite panda teddy.

'She will need a good wash', said mum.

'Can I help?' asked Anna.

'Of course, you can', said mum, 'it's good to have our family all back together again'.

Anna rested her head on mum's shoulder and breathed a very big sigh of relief. She could now sleep knowing that whatever happened, Mandy would find a way back to her. Anna knew that Mandy would always remain her favourite panda teddy, and she would keep her with her, for as long as she was still a little girl. Anna also knew that even when she grew up and became too old for Mandy, she would still love her just as much as she did right then, no matter how scraggly she became.

Mandy was found. Her heart felt like it would explode with joy and relief at being reunited with her beloved Anna. She thought about everything that had happened since that first moment when she was blown off the deck and in to the sea. She thought about the whale and her kindness, the dolphins, the creatures at the meadow, and of course the turtle. She would never forget their kindness and would think of them often, as long as she had stuffing in her weary little head. Mandy also thought about all the adventures she'd had and how she'd been so proud to tell the others at the bottom of the bed. What sights she had seen. But this time she was not so proud, for she realised that her thrill for adventure had landed her in this situation. Her curiosity had gotten the better of her on that fateful day, and taken her so far away from her family that she was nearly lost forever. Mandy also realised that her determination had kept her going, willing her back to her family. For she had literally crossed an ocean to be with her Anna, who would remain her true friend, always and forever...

THE END

Join Mandy on another adventure!

Out Now

Printed in Great Britain
by Amazon